Let's Say HI to Friends Who FLY!

by
MO WILLEMS

Come on!

Balzer + Bray
An Imprint of HarperCollins Publishers

Can you fly, Bee the Bee?

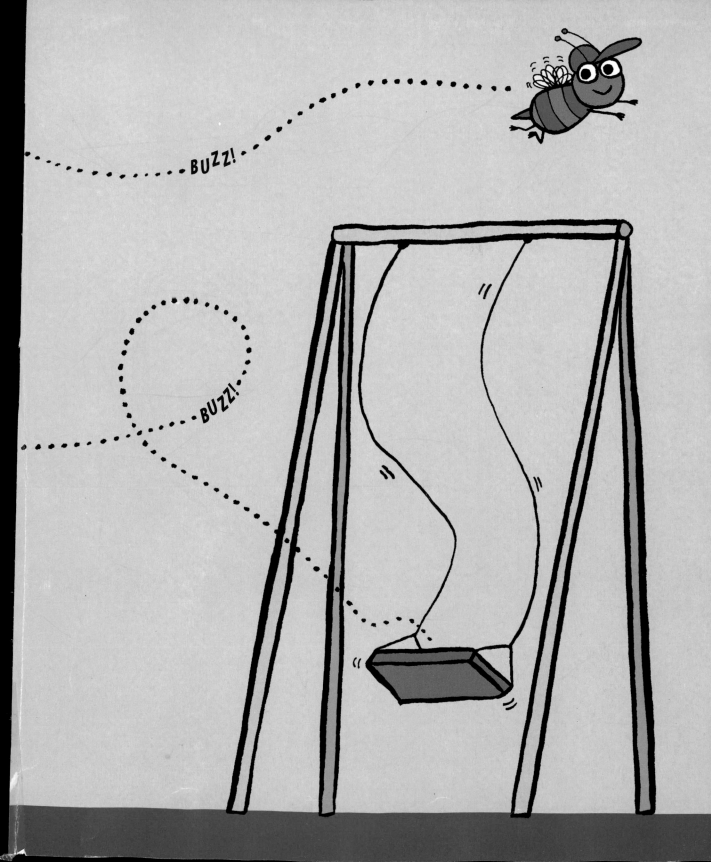

Can you fly, Bird the Bird?

Can you fly,
Bat the Bat?

Who else can fly?

Can YOU fly,
Rhino the Rhino?

Let's ALL fly!

For my new neighbors,

avian and others

Let's Say Hi to Friends Who Fly!

Copyright © 2010 by Mo Willems

Printed in the U.S.A.

www.harpercollinschildrens.com

Library of Congress Cataloging-in-Publication Data

Willems, Mo.

Let's say hi to friends who fly! / Mo Willems. — 1st ed.

p.   cm.

Summary: An exuberant cat cheers on her friends as they demonstrate whether or not they can fly.

ISBN 978-0-06-172842-6 (trade bdg.) — ISBN 978-0-06-172846-4 (lib. bdg.)

[1. Cats—Fiction. 2. Flight—Fiction. 3. Animals—Fiction.] I. Title. II. Title: Let us say hi to friends who fly.

PZ7.W65535Let 2010   2008051713

[E]—dc22   CIP

                                                                                              AC

Typography by Martha Rago

10 11 12 13 14 LPR 10 9 8 7 6 5 4 3 2 1

❖

First Edition